FGHIJK
QRSTU
ABCDE
LMNOP

Wisconsin is filled with fantastic and beautiful things to see and do. Just follow the **A, B, C's**, there is an amazing adventure waiting for you!

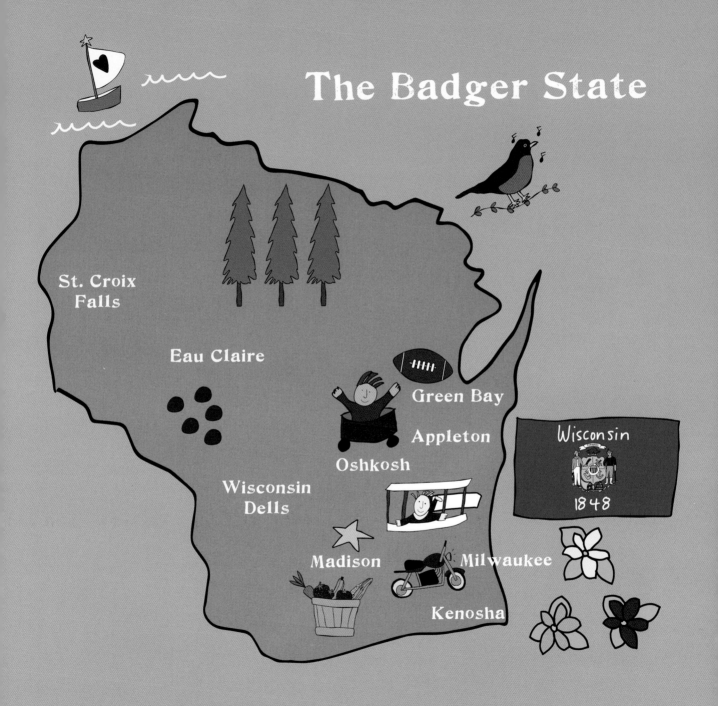

The Badger State

St. Croix
Falls

Eau Claire

Green Bay

Appleton

Oshkosh

Wisconsin
Dells

Wisconsin
1848

Madison

Milwaukee

Kenosha

A is for our amusement park at Bay Beach. The rides will make you holler and yell!

B

is for **Bookworm Gardens,** where playful adventure and creativity dwell.

C is for cranberry.

It's our deliciously tangy state fruit!

D is for **Devil's Lake** State Park.

Come splash around in your swimsuit!

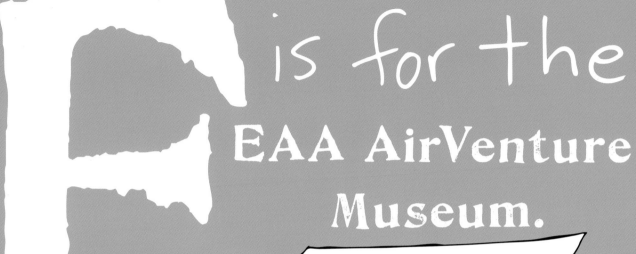

E is for the EAA AirVenture Museum.

See historic planes that were flown by the best.

F is for such fun festivals

like Polish Fest, Irish Fest and the awesome Oktoberfest.

G is for the city of **Green Bay,**

where the National Railroad Museum and its awesome trains are.

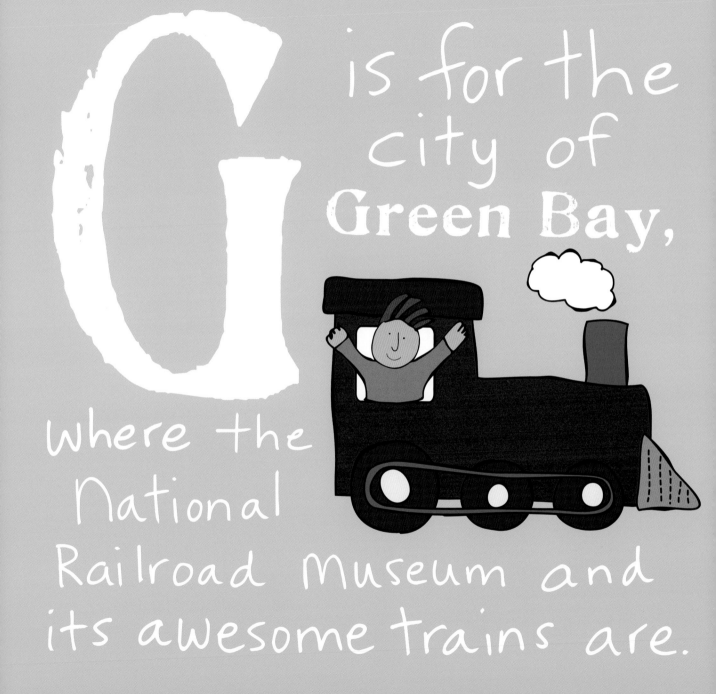

H is for the Harley-Davidson Museum.

These motorcycles are great and the fastest by far.

I is for our **Ice Age National Scenic Trail,** a beautiful place to play.

J

is for **jumping** into Lake Superior on a nice, hot summer day.

K  is for kringle.

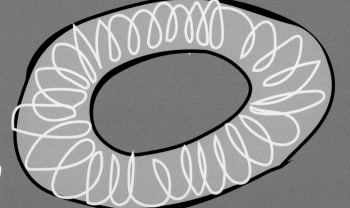

Our yummy
State pastry
has such pizzazz!

L

is for **Lambeau Field**,

'cause touchdowns have lots of razzmatazz!

M

is for the Farmer's Market in **Madison.**

You'll find treats like cherries, corn and cupcakes.

N

is for the **Northern Highland,** filled with awesome ancient forests and natural glacial lakes.

O is for **Olbrich Botanical Gardens.**

See gorgeous flowers and plants galore.

P is for **polka.**

Our playful and lively state dance is one that we all adore!

Q is for **quietly** gazing at stars that shine over the Central Plain at night.

R

is for the **robin.** We just

love to hear our state bird singing at morning's first light.

S

is for **Swiss, string or Shepherd's Blend.**

Our state is known for its award-winning cheese.

T is for the **tremendous** snowstorms that cover up our land, houses, cars and trees!

U is for **upriver** on the Mississippi, where we float along as if in a dream.

V is for **viola.**

Our state flower blooms in bright colors like purple, blue and cream.

W **is for the Wisconsin Maritime Museum,** where we learn sailing takes a special skill and touch.

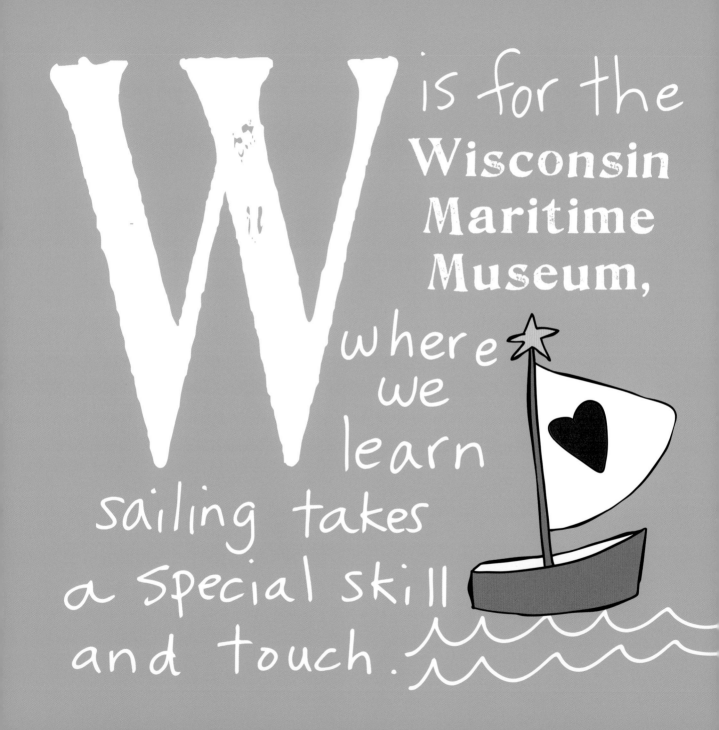

X is for XOXO

because we love all of the wonderful things our state has to offer oh so much!

Y is for our **yummy** state drink.

Have a glass of milk with cookies every day!

Z is for our **zoo** in Milwaukee, where we see the animals run and play.

adventure

an end,
can go
A and
again!

Sandra Magsamen is a best-selling and award-winning artist, author and designer whose meaningful and message-driven art has touched millions of lives, one heart at a time. She loves to travel and has had many awesome adventures around the world. For now, she lives happily and artfully in Vermont with her family and their dog, Olive.

A big thank you to my amazing studio team of Hannah Barry and Karen Botti. Their creativity, research tenacity and spirit of adventure have been invaluable as we crafted the ABC adventure series.

Sandra Magsamen

Text and illustrations © 2016 Hanny Girl Productions, Inc. www.sandramagsamen.com
Exclusively represented by Mixed Media Group, Inc. NY, NY.
Cover and internal design © 2016 by Sandra Magsamen

Sourcebooks and the colophon are registered trademarks of Sourcebooks, Inc.

Published by Sourcebooks Jabberwocky, an imprint of Sourcebooks, Inc.
P.O. Box 4410, Naperville, Illinois 60567-4410
(630) 961-3900
Fax: (630) 961-2168
www.sourcebooks.com

Library of Congress Cataloging-in-Publication data is on file with the publisher.

Source of Production: Leo Paper, Heshan City, Guangdong Province, China
Date of Production: November 2015
Run Number: 5004882

Printed and bound in China.
LEO 10 9 8 7 6 5 4 3 2 1

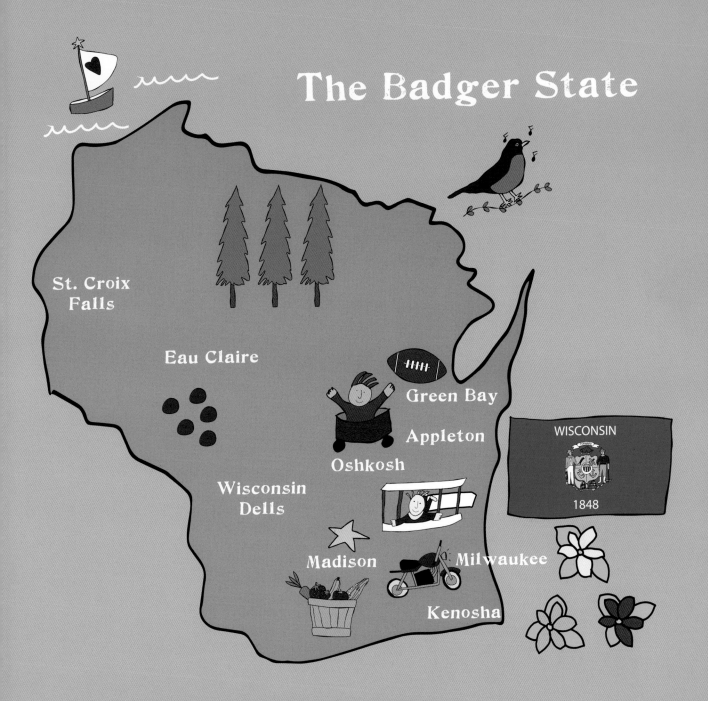

The Badger State

St. Croix Falls

Eau Claire

Green Bay

Appleton

Oshkosh

Wisconsin Dells

WISCONSIN

1848

Madison

Milwaukee

Kenosha

ABCDE

LMNOP

VWXYZ

FGHIJK